AF541147

Catastrophic World

Kanav Sharma

INVINCIBLE PUBLISHERS

First Printing: 2020

ISBN: 978-93-89600-41-4

Invincible Publishers

Registered Address: 201A, SAS Tower, Sector 38, Gurgaon - 122003

Phone - +91-124-4034247, +91 9355675555

www.invinciblepublishers.com

Acknowledgment

'Thank you' is a very small word for the gratitude I feel for the loved ones in my life.

I am highly indebted to God Almighty for showering his blessings upon me, for always holding my hand and guiding me, and for always being my protector.

The grandparents are angels who sprinkle stardust on their grandchildren. For me, it's my Dadaji and Nanaji, who send their blessings to me from heaven - my sincere gratitude to them. And, a big thanks to my lovely and gorgeous Dadi and Nani for their unconditional love and care.

I am really fortunate to have the best parents in the world. No matter what the situation is, no matter what blunders I make, and no matter how many times I have troubled them; they have not only supported me but have also been my rock of strength at all times.

And my biggest thanks is for the sweetest person on this earth – my sister. She always believed in me, when no one else did. She thought I could do it when everyone else thought I was bound to be doomed. I don't say it much, but I love you the most, my sister. Thank you so much for being there for me.

The book would have been difficult to complete without the help of my honest critic, supporter, and motivator - Mrs. Raminder Kaur.

A special thanks to the team of Invincible Publishers for helping me in bringing my second book to reality.

Last but not least, I thank everyone who has been the part of my journey, has taught me something, or has been a supporter and a motivator.

I thank you all.

Preface

In one of my Biology classes, when the teacher was talking about the structure of the brain, describing it as something which has cerebrum, cerebellum, medulla and a ton of other things, I started wondering about it; I had always thought of it as a 'tangled web of thoughts'.

It's the brain that perceives messages from the five-sense organs and then processes them, thereby producing thoughts and feelings.

For me, the human brain is like a MAZE; you start from one end and have to go on a roundabout journey experiencing different flavors of the cuisine called 'life'. After reaching the other end, it is a journey that enlightens an individual and awakens his innovative side which gets you to learn what you learn in this MAZE, and what shapes your life.

Each person's takeaways from this journey are different. Some see the glass half-empty and some as half-full.

Whatever I have learned till now is that the glass is half-full of water and half-filled with air. And that's what is reflected in my poems; in my first book 'Implicit Feelings of a Teenager' and now this book, 'Catastrophic World'.

Sky

The sky is so blue
Looking through I have no clue
No clue of time
Silent as mime
How lovely it looks with birds flying high
And that auspicious moment when the sun says bye
The moon looks ravishing every day
Always open to interpretation and changing phases
– a reflection of life is what it conveys
The stars when they flicker
Sometimes makes you want to linger
The solace of sky providing opulence in abundance
And the feeling of exhilaration is always high

Oceans

Never ending blue oceans
Peacefully handle emotions.
So calm that voice is
When water pecks land with a delectable kiss
So many secrets buried under
To know you have to go deep into the wonders
To beautiful creatures they're a home
Ocean's mystic life is yet to be shown
So serene at sunset
No rust no stress in mind
That is so alluring when oceans are benevolent
Sitting beside ocean alleviates you
And you will fall in love with it without a clue

Cries

How are cries a part of human nature?

Tears fall coz of happiness anger sadness

Or even while watching a picture

Humans have so many emotions

But why only smiles and cries make them look beautiful?

A baby cries when he is born

Probably because of missed opportunities in past

Tears for him are words –

Discomfort need or hunger

They convey

Black Blue Green or Grey –

Eyes of all colors filled with clear liquid.

How beautiful they look

How powerful yet so helpless

So exotic yet so miserable

So expressive yet so mysterious

Not always bad

The first drop that falls on the cheek

Makes you more of a human who is not weak
You cry when you're frustrated by things
A placidity to your soul is what it brings

Don't Lose Hope

When darkness and failure surround your soul
Know that you have to stand bold
When you don't have an option
Know that you can cross the failure and congestion
When things don't seem to work out
Know that you don't have to shout
When everything is a mess
Know that you have the power of a king or a queen like in chess
When no one stands with you
Know that you are your own crew
When you feel tired and still cannot sleep
Know that what makes you unique
When you try to fake
Know that you won't have meaning for god's sake
When you give up
Know that you'll be stuck
When you work hard
Know that you'll be a success and you'll stand apart

When you start doubting yourself
Know that that will be the day when you'll ask for help
When you stay strong
Know that everything will stay with you for long

Life's Loop

How weird it is when someone dies
People mourning echoes screams and cries
The dead so composed tranquil and placid
Their sumptuous minds come to rest
And their quiet heart silence is not the best
Their memories are all that's left
In your mind a precious crest
And as time passes
Their memories fade a little
But their thoughts in your mind are still as green as grasses
Their resplendent face is always in your mind
And you want them back
Because your love towards them is always alive and fresh
Unique in its own kind

My Biggest Mistake

I don't know why I am in doubt
Why did I ever let you go
Was it a phase
Or was it me who couldn't face
The situation of deep care
I thought we had gone too far
Making myself believe that it was our stars
But it was me who was scared
Although you still cared
Today I have realized my mistake
My heart and feelings are at stake
You have all the rights to hate me
I'll pull everything together especially myself
And all you have to do is see
I don't know why I can't stop
Falling into love again
I know we have fallen apart
Because of my unreasonable fear of sharing myself
I wish could once again I start

Take it all the way it's meant to last
I've seen myself disintegrate into pieces
Leaving me shattered when you are gone
I want to once again experience the magic
Once again want to feel alive
Once again want to sail the boat of life

The Unknowns

We sleep at night peacefully
Living a life of luxury
What about those who do not have a roof?
What about those walking barefoot?
Seeing people in miserable conditions
What we do is only curse the system
Mere words no actions
Wearing branded clothes
We disregard the shabby faces
Many people don't treat them well
But some are angels pulling them out of hell
All hypocrites benefit from their sorrow
Giving them hope of a new morrow
In the end leave them high and dry-
To ponder and to cry
Going to own sheltered cocoon
Promise to change their lives soon

What Nature

Under this blue sky
I see some laugh and cry
How beautiful this world is
Having so many hues
To please
How beautiful those birds are
Open their wings
And fly far and far
Deep the woods are
Not much place for anyone when it's dark
There is so much to appreciate
More than what you create
The sun brightens up the day
The moon calms the day with grace
What I have gained so far
I see this world as an art
So many things to learn
So much happiness and smiles to earn

Long Roads

How beautiful those roads are
Leading to places that are enchanting and far
The roads with blue skies
Where butterfly flies
The long green trees
With sweet buzz of bees
How beautiful those roads are
Smooth during the rain showers
Empty roads have deep silence
Feels so peaceful and belonging to no alliance
Some leading through mountains
Some through rivers
Some through woods
Some through deserts
Keep us away from stressful hazards

Undeniable

What are we?
Is not the question
Where are we?
Living in this place
Full of life
With people adjusting in limited space
But what have we done to it?
Made it worse
We say we give the best gifts to others
But this is the worst you are
Giving to your children as adults
We have destroyed it to an extent
Where it is non-fixable
Everything happening here is UNDENIABLE
Deforestation weather changes forest fires
You are nothing but adult liars
Lying to us about a world
So peaceful and calm
But what we hear every day is a forest burned causing a

lot of harm
You are not only ‘ending’ life
But its existence
Why not stab us before bringing us to life?
Because you have made this world hell already
Because we are not ready
To live in the trash you have made that pretty heavy

Two Strangers

We were one
Now we are two different people standing apart
I still wish to begin right from the start
Those shiny eyes of yours
Opened all my heart's doors
I remember the first time we met I was dazed
I can still feel the sweetness and love
Falling out of that kiss
I had never thought it would ill end without a goodbye
You left me my heart was abashed confound and fazed
A memory train
Takes me through a lot of pain
When someone asks me to describe you
All I have in mind is 'I loved you'
'I love you' and will always love you

Kanav Sharma

The Coldest Winters

I am waiting for long
For this winter to be gone
It's pleasant and sometimes mushy
With dark clouds hovering around
Leaving me perplexed
Winters are little complex
It is a ride of déjà vu
Taking me through the memory lane
Of the days when
Winters were all about laziness
Lying in the sun enjoying the hot soup
Or holding the blankets tight
Munching the peanuts
Gone are the beautiful days
It's cold and foggy
But memories of winters never fade
Even the coldest winters leave you
Hypnotized and the memories
Are stored to be cherished

Words And Worlds

The deep complex words
Coming out of your mouth
Make me anxious and panicky
So I shout.
There is subtle pureness in your voice
I am in dilemma is it wise to make that choice?
You said a few words to keep
But I know what they mean
It took me to a long road
Analyzing thoughts that were lovely and deep
But the game of words is tricky
And I want to stay normal not pricky

Calmness

Looking through the window
Enjoying the sunset and the trees' shadow
So calm that feeling is
When the hills and the sun kiss
The sound of the valley is mystifying
I feel like losing myself
But still there is something
That is missing
That is the smile on the faces
Which when absent everyone cries
The colors become faded
And everything seems like it is shaded
There will be a day when sad corpus will fall
The bad memories within will crawl
And a new sun will rise
Spreading happiness and joys
Through its glorifying rays

Our Fault

I don't know why there's silence all around
Everything has gone pale disintegration of self surrounds
Why do I have hopes
When in the end everything shatters?
How come I feel it's been too long?
We both ran out of love and care
For keeping the bond alive none of us was that strong
We thought running out of love is just a phase
But deep down the heart we both knew we weren't meant for the long chase
I am still confused that why I never felt sad for us
It can either be me who is used to efforts half hearted from both sides
I still do think about you
I wish 'you thinking about me' was true
I don't know why I still feel I miss you
Why my mind is full of thoughts about you you and you?

Pretty Day

It's such a warm pretty day
It's bright and sun kissed they say
Its warmth
Making me feel at home
The birds taking flight in the sky
All the flowers blooming to their full glory
And everyone smile even though they are shy
The leaves seem to be lively and green
I ask until now where this day had been?
Everything is so beautiful so serene
Nature is bountiful and giving and not at all mean
That's what sharing and caring feels
Making your life just like this warm pretty day

Winters

I don't know why there is a sudden calmness in winters
I don't know why there is satisfaction in granny's mode sweaters
I don't know why there is no feeling that is overwhelming
I don't know why there are smiles which get more charming
I don't know why the dust settles itself on the ground
I don't know why the wind makes such sound
I don't know why the mother's hug is warmer
I don't know why the person you love looks closer
I don't know why I love you even though it's hurting
I don't know why the feeling of silence is there
But I guess
It's because winters are here here here

Worship

You think your prayers are the key to your freedom
But that's just how people own you exploit you and take you away
From your wisdom
I am not crazy enough
To believe it as distortion of reality
Which although not impossible is quite tough
We all are at perpetual war with each other
But we don't stop noticing
The flows pointing fingers playing the blame game
The quest to move on
Is not delusional
But is like all of us judging each other
The rubrics from our past
The adherence to so many feelings
You keep them and you'll go mad
You let them out you are insane
The society won't leave you alone

Deletion

That stage of Deletion
The stage I have to make a single decision
I won't be psyched by a moment of hesitation
When I have to choose between yes or no
Yes means ridding myself of all my memories
No means holding on to them
And keep reminding myself all those stories
I have to make a decision
Cause the anxiety isn't going away anymore
It's just there
I am in a chaotic condition
That is leading me and my wisdom to the path of separation

I Don't Know

I don't know what's wrong

I don't know why I am suddenly not strong

I don't know why I am having rush of emotions

I don't know why I am not able to pull out my real appearance

I don't know why I go all mad at myself

I don't know why I am not ready to take anybody's help

I don't know why I see everything only in chaos

I don't know why someone in me is gone to the other side

I don't know why I wanna run away and hide

I don't know why I start missing you in the middle of the nights

I don't know why the memory is peaceful as flying the colorful kites

I Wish

I wish I could have been what they wanted me to be

I wish I could have been more serene

I wish I could have been more honest

I wish I could have been more disciplined

I wish I could have had the power of acceptance

I wish I could have pulled out that long carried heaviness

I wish I could have made things work out

I wish I could have never lied

I wish I could have never cried

I wish I could have done that

I wish I could have stood against the bad

I wish I could have never lost my morals

I wish I could have never forgotten my roots

I wish I could have worked harder

I wish I could have been courageous

I wish I could have been able to turn the clock
I wish I could have been able to change the past
I wish I could have been able to clean the board
I wish I could have been able to start afresh

Human Minds

Human Mind is a dangerous place
We see or make things we say
For recognition but it kills the inner you
The decision we take isn't sometimes true
The darkest fears become the reality
This only leads to cruelty
How hard it is to control your emotions
Which makes you sad and leads to bad notions
It is about dreaming reality
But not any filtered motion of sincerity
Hope is not a word
It's just a way to please our inner self
Trying to attain satisfaction is human nature
But there is no way a human attains everything
The day the thirsty human satisfies himself
Will be the day human mind is out of the box and kept on the shelf

Me Time

The time when I ask myself question
Is the time I am the quietest
The time when I have lots of hesitations
Is the time when I am losing my calm
The time when I see someone ignore me
Is the time when I let them do the harm
The time when I remember the old times
Is the time I regret the most
The time when I think about the people I love
Is the time when I am weak
The time when everything is fine
Is the time I cannot sleep
The time I realize how habitual I've become to disappointment
Is the time I feel so ashamed
The time I tell the truth
Is the time I feel blamed
The time when I realize something keeps going on
Is the time when I realize my life is on the right track

What Are We

Finding answers to what you are about
Can make you end your self doubt
After every failure we make resolutions
We try to take all long time precautions
And again we see ourselves in dark clouds
We try again and give our souls a loud shout
Finding faults in everything is what humans do
Asking illogical questions from a five year old "why is the sky blue?"
We humans are never prepared for failures in childhood
We are taught to stay strong stand firm and be prepared for success
Never taught to face the harsh and struggling reality
It's as if we are all set to dig up our own graves
Most humans destroy mental health
Cause what they are prepared for
Is success and a fake dream of lots and lots of wealth

It is not wrong to stand strong
It is not wrong to gain self confidence
But when it gets to your head
You will end up with nothing but a shout for help

Aimless

I am not disturbed
But a little perplexed
I feel I have no path
Or a goal to aim for
How can someone be so confused?
I have no idea what to choose
I want to work on something I am proud of
The road won't be lost
And I don't need anyone to push or promote
I myself have the courage
I have the potential
To do something that I feel is essential
All I need to do is widen up my horizon
And throw away all the pessimism

Live A Life

How silly we humans are
Wanting something
Doing something else
Confused in our own thoughts
Not trusting our own decisions
So we don't give it a shot
Hope we grow up soon enough
To not to regret all our stuff
We go the opposite way
Till everything we have planned goes astray
Cause we all know the final conclusion
For which there is no confusion
Cause it's the sudden stop to all our senses
All you will remember is the scent of a flower
Which you smelled
When you were ten
All you will be able to feel will be your mother's first touch
All you will be able to remember is that there was still much

Still much to see
Still much to laugh
Still much to cry
Still much to sigh
But not soon enough to die
Die with regrets
Cause you never tried what you wanted
Cause your thoughts and dreams were always haunted
Haunted by the people who discouraged you
Haunted by the people who spoke against you
Haunted by the fear of failure
So do what your mind tells you to do
Find your logic and your satisfaction
And don't just survive to get through
Live a life with no regrets
Live a life you dream of
Live a life you deserve
Live a life
Cause you are worth it

Rules And Humans

Why is there a sudden rush of emotions?
I am tired of these tiring sad notions
I don't know why there is a charm in the rules of humankind
This invisible code of chaos hiding somewhere in my mind
The menacing face of order
Makes me wanna cry out even louder
The things from the past are haunting me
I don't know why it's divided into three
My family my fears and you
I tried everything just to get through
Every time I found myself repenting over and over
Not realizing every time I sat with regret
I found myself closer
Closer to everything I never ever thought of
I agree all we had wasn't made in one day
Wish I could go to the start is all I pray

Jealousy

Why is jealousy raiding my heart and mind?
I thought I was pure and kind
I am not what I thought
I guess I was over confident
Now all those actions I repent
Someone else took my place
But that doesn't make me out of the race
I know where I was wrong
Now I am clear about the path I belong
I'll be someone they cannot expect
Because the difficult path leads to respect

Shadows

The old trees casting their shadows
On the canyons deep down
The sudden phases of clouds frown
The way everything goes subtle
And birds go out to play
Seem so beautiful
But the shadows on the canyon
Seem to hold me back
A sudden realization of all the mistakes
And in all the motivation you gained breaks
The shattered glass seems like pieces of my life
Shattered broken yet glimmering with an inner shine

Brains

Half dead Half alive
We all try to survive
Things like anxiety and stress surrounding us
The brains are all in a mush
Trying to fight for something we don't know
"We are all ready for it"
We try to show
Not able to take a risk
Scared of not being called brisk
Filling up the pages of notebooks
We don't realize
We're all some dumb dummies hanging on a hook
Let your imagination fly
Let your brain stumble and try –
Try to adapt
Try to discover you away from all your fears

Crowd

Varied faces running in one direction
In search of things
Without realizing all the repercussions
Having a single point of view
Never looking the other way
The memories and creativity outgrew
Trying to lay hands on something big
Forgetting about the dream gig
Lying to themselves they walk
With eyes closed
They all talk
Passion for one thing driving them crazy
Not sacrificing
For a dream so hazy
All running a mad rat race
Crowd becoming another face

Ambition

Synonym of life
We all have an idea about future
For which we all strive
If you have no ambition
Then you already have lost your vision
Mind is divided in two parts
One the ideology brain
One that calculates what to carry to the cart
Just like hope drives us all
Ambition drives our soul
Otherwise we'll all be just mindless freaks
Walking here and there like Zombies
With no goal and no mission.

World

It's not limited to human life
But is more than us
Or the wildlife
We all get out of our bed in the morning
Feeling nothing
Nothing
Seems to groove us
Until it's something extreme
Because we don't seem to care
And get on with the life's bus
When two things bump into each other

You

Words that come out of your mouth
Stays in my mind
Like when you shout
I remember your face
With an absurd expression
No one can decipher
I see your mind and that's a beauty
When I talk to you
Everything seems so pretty
A thousand things hit me every day
While I just stand there
Trying to make you stay

Heart

We are under surveillance of everyone

Cause we open up

Thinking that he or she is the one

Some don't some do

With a hope

Hope brings pain to you

Subconsciously we don't realize what we are going through

And consciously we don't care about the future that lingers and then blows away

In the black and white shades of grey

A lot of strength to take risks comes through

The winners are those whose heart is pure and true

Let's make a start

Let your positive beat resonate with your heart

Thinking

Blank expression to the sky
We dream to be a superhuman and fly
Fly away from things we hate
And live in a world we create
Fantasizing of being successful we make plans
We forget we are acting like a fool
Our dreams could be a reality
When we start working
And face the cruelty
Our brain feels good when we dream
But it's just like sunscreen lotion
Protecting us from reality which is going unseen

Questions

What is the art of questioning?
Asking the right one at the right time
Questioning things not properly functioning
It's a way to control
Control the crowd by not being scared
Understanding what is the right question
Can change your whole life without any repercussion
Because you might not find the right answer
But learn and create something to solve that mystery
Your brain interprets everything you see or read
And questioning is the part of the process so discrete

Materialistic Things

Small things drive us
Give us hope
To be something with no fuss
How Why?
It's so interesting to look at those things
And relate them to yourself
Cause it makes us feel like we are not hanging on a string
It could be a book a mix tape a photo or something trifle
That takes us to a moment
Nobody likes to hang in the middle
Because there is uncertainty
And that 'thing' solves your riddle

Skin

Colors don't matter

But your thoughts your deeds

Can make you rise or shatter

All of us think of ourselves honest and true

But no one is happy with life in their own skin

When will we be comfortable with ourselves as humans and not just flash?

The day when all is gone

Gone are your regrets your happiness

Your family your money everything

When you are alone and think about yourself

Is the day when you will get a response?

Response from within

Telling you that's the real

And that will set everything right

Secrets

Thoughts we all keep
In our minds
Away from
Steep falls of trust
We see ourselves as secret keepers
The most secretive thing
Is the most genuine thing about you
You don't know how many are they
Many or few
Deep in us we have an image of ourselves
That we want to see
And that image differentiates us from fake and realistic
Those secrets are no different than thoughts
Both of them stay with you

Thoughts

We see something and we think about it
Sometimes it's things sometimes memories from past
Sometimes moments of present
Sometimes flashes from future
Thoughts give ambition gives us ideas
It's a beautiful process by our brain
Increasing our chances to give better with no strain
Giving a thought to something
Shows how you are a human
Cause every thought is unique and brings a great transformation

Decision

We take a thousand decisions every day
From what to eat
To how to breathe
But the big question is-
How to make the right one?
How to be sure of this?
Like 2 sides of coin
Like a dice we roll
We are not scared of taking a decision
But we are in dilemma
Our brain tries to find its pros and cons
That is the only reflex action not bruised
Sometimes we just go with instincts
We lose we win
But it's the expression we get which is distinct

Why?

This happy place is formed
With all the stars the moon the sun
Around us
Then why can't we wake up feeling good
It's because we know
Even though we are surrounded by people
We're still lonely and filled with sorrow
Past regrets a feeling of being left out
Keeps us up all night
Why?
Because we have given up all hope
Hope to live instead of surviving